George Keate

The monument in Arcadia: a dramatic poem, in two acts

George Keate

The monument in Arcadia: a dramatic poem, in two acts

ISBN/EAN: 9783337306052

Printed in Europe, USA, Canada, Australia, Japan

Cover: Foto ©Andreas Hilbeck / pixelio.de

More available books at **www.hansebooks.com**

THE

MONUMENT IN ARCADIA:

A

DRAMATIC POEM,

IN TWO ACTS.

By GEORGE KEATE, Esq.

ET IN ARCADIA EGO——

LONDON:
PRINTED FOR J. DODSLEY, IN PALL-MALL.
MDCCLXXIII.

T O

THE RIGHT HONOURABLE

LADY VISCOUNTESS PRIMEROSE,

THIS POEM

IS INSCRIBED,

IN GRATEFUL TESTIMONY

OF THE FRIENDSHIP

WITH WHICH SHE HAS LONG HONOURED

HER LADYSHIP'S

MOST OBLIGED

AND AFFECTIONATE SERVANT,

GEO. KEATE.

ADVERTISEMENT.

THE ABBÉ DU BOS, *in his Critical Reflec-*
tions on Poetry and Painting, *mentions with*
great Encomium a Picture of POUSSIN, *wherein*
are reprefented fome ARCADIAN Shepherds and
Shepherdeffes, *who contemplate a Monument,* *on*
which they read this Infcription, ET IN ARCADIA
EGO.

He

He supposes an Object so unexpected to have damped the Festivity of the Hour, and adds, L'on ne voit plus sur leurs Visages à travers l'Affliction, qui s'en empare, que les Restes d'une Joïe expirante.

I much doubt whether in the above Quotation the ingenious Critic does not give a Merit to the Artist, which the Art never yet attained. The Changes of the human Countenance are occasionally as quick as the Operation of Thought; and the Rapidity of their Succession can awaken in a Spectator such a Combination of Ideas, as to produce almost instantaneously a correspondent Passion.

PAINTING

PAINTING *can but half tell her Story.---The Pencil even under the happiest Guidance, must be confined to a single Action, nor can express more than the present Sentiment.----To unveil external Appearances, and to paint that previous Disposition of the Mind which fixes them, and which can magnify familiar Events into Effects of Moment, is an elder Sister's Province, and the peculiar Property of the* MUSE.

It was this Reflection that induced me to form on the Subject of POUSSIN's *Picture, the following little Piece, which is probably of too serious a Cast for public Representation.---I do not recollect that the Moral it conveys has yet been delivered from the Stage; for though* HOPE *remains to us the comfort-*

able

able *Balance* for THE FATAL INGREDIENTS OF THE Box, *yet no Truth appears more obvious, than that the Fervor of an indulged Imagination may involve us in* FANCIED *Diſtreſſes, as painful to the Heart as* moſt *of the* REAL *ones which the World prepares for us.*

Perſons of the Drama.

DORASTUS, a rich Shepherd, living as a Hermit.

LYSANDER, a young SPARTAN, Lover of EUPHEMIA.

MUSIDORUS, an ARCADIAN Shepherd.

EUPHEMIA, betrothed to LYSANDER.

DELIA, Friend to EUPHEMIA.

DAPHNE,

LAURA, } Daughters of MUSIDORUS.

ARCADIANS.

Scene, ARCADIA.

THE

THE

MONUMENT IN ARCADIA:

A DRAMATIC POEM.

ACT I.

SCENE—*A beautiful Prospect of* ARCADIA; *Shepherds Dwellings dis-persed at a Distance, and a Wood on one Side.*

Enter LYSANDER, EUPHEMIA, *and* DELIA.

LYSANDER.

THANKS to the Gods! our cheerful Steps at last
    Have reach'd these happy Climes; where refug'd Virtue,
'Midst laughing Vales, o'er-arch'd by cloudless Skies,
Enjoys a calm Retreat. And now, lov'd Maid!
Whom I have follow'd, and would follow still
To Earth's remotest Bounds; 'tis Time to claim

That

That bright Reward, which, before DELIA here,

Your lov'd Companion DELIA, you have fworn,

Soon as my Voice had welcom'd your Arrival,

Should crown my willing Service.

EUPHEMIA.

Gen'rous Youth!

Whofe fond Compliance with a Maid's Requeft

Has led you far from home; the Boon you afk

Will poorly pay your Virtues; take my Hand,

And know I give it but to pledge a Heart

By ev'ry Title yours.

DELIA.

Unfhaken, long

Remain this Union!— Now! EUPHEMIA, now

Behold your Hopes accomplifh'd!— Breathe we not

A purer Air? And does not this bright Scene,

Which opens round us, realize the Truth

Of all ARANTHE faid?

EUPHEMIA.

E U P H E M I A.

It does; it does.
Peace to her Shade!   And, DELIA, we fhall blefs
The friendly Path we trod; though fcarcely yet
LYSANDER knows why I fo long forbore
To crown his Love, and in this diftant Clime
Would only wed.

L Y S A N D E R.

It was enough for me
To know your Wifh; contented to be bleft
On your own Terms.   But oft' I've heard you fay,
Your dying Mother, poor ARANTHE! left
Thefe Counfels in your Ear, with that fad Sigh
Which never more is heard.

E U P H E M I A.

Her Care alone
Rear'd me to what I am; yet I ne'er knew
A Parent's Fondnefs.   She was of ARCADIA;
And when the SPARTAN Arms, with fierce Defcent,

Sought

Sought thefe defencelefs Shades, was forc'd away
With other Captives. Then, all pale with Tears,
Left Violence fhould feize what Choice deny'd,
She gave the Plund'rer, what he afk'd, her Hand,
And yielded to his Wifh.—Vows thus conftrain'd
Ne'er draw down Bleffings. Fifteen tedious Years
She felt a lordly Hufband's rigid Sway;
Till Fate diffolv'd her Bondage, and reftor'd
Her Liberty.

LYSANDER.

Euphemia, you relate
What moves my Wonder; for till now, I deem'd
You were Aranthe's Child.

EUPHEMIA.

I thought fo too:
But mark the Sequel. Freedom came too late :
Worn by Diffimulation's irkfome Tafk
For Years repeated, flow-confuming Care
Subdu'd at laft her Frame. Arcadia's Vales

She

She now no more could viſit; that fond Hope

Through long Captivity ſuſtain'd the Soul,

Which ſunk to find it loſt.

LYSANDER.

Not long the Mourner

Surviv'd her Huſband?

EUPHEMIA.

Scarcely half the Space

Of ten ſad Moons.   The Lamp of Life each Day

Burnt fainter; and a ſudden Stroke its Light

Almoſt extinguiſhing, ſhe call'd me to her,

And bade me bring the Friend whom moſt I lov'd,

My DELIA, with me.   To our Ears ſhe then,

By interrupted Words with Pain brought forth,

Unlock'd her Heart;—told me, a Mother's Name

Was but aſſum'd, that he whom ſhe eſpous'd

Might treat me gently; that my infant Years

Were to her Care confided; that her All

She had bequeath'd me; and her dying Wiſh

Was

Was, that, when Time fhould favor the Intent,

I'd feek ARCADIA.——— " If, my Child!" fhe cry'd,

" Thy Lot be Happinefs, 'twill meet thee there;

" Be Hope thy Guide: The righteous Gods, perhaps

" May there reftore".———But what—was all conceal'd;

For Death that Inftant feiz'd her Pow'rs of Speech,

And left me loft in Darknefs and Diftrefs.

D E L I A.

Nor till her Spirit fled, ceas'd fhe to fix,

Though Utt'rance was deny'd, on my fair Friend

Looks forcible as Language.—We have fearch'd,

Where'er Conjecture wings its dubious Flight,

To trace her Meaning, or defcry from whence

EUPHEMIA drew her Birth; but ev'ry Path

Perplex'd and tangled, ftill in Darknefs ends.

L Y S A N D E R.

Some Caufe forbade, or fhe had ne'er fo long

Conceal'd the Story, which her parting Breath

Could not enough difclofe. But fay, my Love,

Did

Did not ARANTHE oft' at other Times

Difcourfe the Beauties of her native Land,

The more to tempt you to this Pilgrimage ?

EUPHEMIA.

Oh, frequent ! frequent !   It was oft' her Subject,

And fhe would tell fuch Wonders of ARCADIA,

So boaft its joyous Skies, where Love, where Truth,

And fair Simplicity reign'd undifturb'd,

That all entranc'd I heard her, and my Soul

Dwelt on her Story, till it pin'd to fee

Thefe Heav'n-diftinguifh'd Regions.—To myfelf,

In fecret, then I vow'd, that I would ne'er

But in ARCADIA wed.—It was for this

ARCADIA was fo oft' my Theme, when firft

You grac'd me with your Notice ; 'twas for this

I hither led you ; and at fome near Shrine

My Vow fhall be confirm'd.

LYSANDER.

Bleft be the Night,

When forth I led you from detefted SPARTA,

Ne'er to behold it more! Detefted SPARTA!

Where the firm Virtue of our rigid Fathers,

Which nerv'd their Arm, and gave th' admiring World

A Line of Heroes, is debas'd by Vice,

Or crufh'd by pow'rful Faction.——To forget

The Cloud that fhades my Country, be my Tafk;

Since thence I've borne a Prize, in whom I view

The Graces of the pureft Times.

EUPHEMIA.

No more!

Already you o'erpay me.

LYSANDER.

Bounteous Maid!

My Tongue would beggar Language, fhould it fpeak

The Tranfport I now feel to call thee mine,

And to enfold thee thus.——Whatever Joys

This Clime fhall offer, they can nothing add

To mine, poffeffing thee.

DELIA.

D E L I A.

Behold! a Troop

Of Swains advancing! Haply, we from them

May gain all due Intelligence.

L Y S A N D E R.

Yet hold!

They seem assembled on some Ceremony;

'Twere best at Distance mark them ;——for a while

Let us withdraw beneath these bow'ring Shades.

[They retire into the Wood.

Enter——MUSIDORUS, DAPHNE, LAURA, *and a Number of* ARCADIAN *Shepherds and Shepherdesses, bearing in their Hands Garlands of Flowers.*

They advance, singing.

C H O R U S.

Give the Hour to sober Pleasures;

Cheerful Hearts are Life's best Treasures:

Let the choral Song go round;

Echo shall our Joys resound.

C   MUSIDORUS.

MUSIDORUS.

Onward Arcadians! bear your flow'ry Wreaths,

Twin'd with the faireſt Sweets of ev'ry Kind

That ſcent the Ev'ning Air, and with them deck

The ſacred Pines of Pan; while the deep Grove

Tells to the diſtant Hills our feſtive Rites.——

'Tis wiſely done to make the moſt of Life:

Whilſt Temp'rance ſits the Guardian of our Sports,

Each grateful Smile that dimples o'er the Cheek

Is Tribute paid the Gods.

FIRST ARCADIAN.

Let ſuch as tread

The buſy Haunts of Men, where Envy ſhoots

Its poiſon'd Arrows, wear their Brow o'ercaſt;

Our Vales are only Witneſſes of Joy,

And Mirth well-authoriz'd; our fertile Soil

A happier Sun-ſhine warms; and the prefs'd Grape

Pouring from Goblets deep its purple Stream,

Drives

Drives off imagin'd Ills, and the cheer'd Mind

Attunes to Harmony.

A I R.

Gloomy Care can ne'er controul

Joys that wait the temp'rate Bowl;

Welcome all its pure Delights,

Blamelefs Days, and peaceful Nights.

In our Cup her radiant Wings

FANCY dips, and brighter fprings;

To her the Pow'r is giv'n

To foar beyond the Pride of Kings,

And form on ev'ry Spot a Heav'n.

LYSANDER, EUPHEMIA, *and* DELIA, *appear from the Wood.*

LYSANDER.

Forgive us Shepherds,

If we as Strangers peradventure prefs

Somewhat abruptly on you.   Wide is fpread

The Fame of your fair Clime; and it hath hither

Allur'd

Allur'd our Steps, inquifitive to learn

That true Simplicity which marks your Lives,

And makes them deem'd fo happy.

MUSIDORUS.

You are welcome

To thefe pacific Shades, and doubly fo

As being Strangers : but if chance you come

From Scenes of artful Life, where Pomp difplays

Its fplendid Fallacies, ours fcarce will charm.———

Yet here Content refides, and rural Eafe ;

With ev'ry Blefling which the bounteous Pan

Beftows on virtuous Toils.

LYSANDER.

Deem not that we

So ill have read the World, that our fool'd Senfe

Is caught by Pageantry.———Nought charms fo much

As the bright Luftre of an upright Mind,

Active, and fteady.———And in lonely Vales,

And Roofs unnotic'd, oft' fuch Virtues dwell

As

As Courts with Pride might boaft; though all unfeen

Their Graces bloom, fave by a circling few,

And Heav'n's approving Eye.

FIRST ARCADIAN.

Your Reas'ning, Youth,

Befpeaks a Mind well tutor'd; and your Chance

Hath thrown you amongft Men, who know to prize

The Heart that points to Virtue.——Freely fhare

Whate'er thefe Plains afford. Say, will you join

Our feftive Rites? Or, rather, do you feek

Reft and Refrefhment?——Long perchance hath been

Your Way; and thefe your fair Companions tire.

LYSANDER.

True——long hath been our Way; but we have made it

Pleafure, not Toil.——You fhall at Leifure know

Whate'er in the fmall Circle of our Lives

May win your Ear. Suffice it now to fay

What beyond Reft, beyond your proffer'd Care,

Sits neareft at my Heart, is, that you guide

3   Our

Our Steps to where, before fome hallow'd Shrine,

This beauteous Maid and I may fwear till Death

A lafting Union.——Long, too long, my Blifs

Hath been delay'd; and tedious feems to creep

Each lazy Minute now, till I can boaft

Alliance with her Virtues.

MUSIDORUS.

Such a Place

Stands in the Covert of yon Wood; be mine

The Tafk to lead you thither.——Leagues of Love

Approv'd by Virtue, from their ftarry Thrones

The Gods behold well pleas'd.——Go you before

My Daughters, and with virgin Hands adorn

The nuptial Altar.——Shepherds, you'll purfue

Your purpos'd Sports: we fhall at Eve rejoin.

[*Exeunt* DAPHNE *and* LAURA.

LYSANDER.

Here, my EUPHEMIA, our long Voyage ends,

Safe in the wifh'd-for Port we ride in Peace,

Anchor'd

Anchor'd by Love and Friendſhip.—Gen'rous Swain!

Your hoſpitable Kindneſs aſks more Praiſe

Than my poor Tongue can give; a Time may come

When I may better ſpeak it.

MUSIDORUS.

Nay! no more;

I act but as I ought.——Benevolence

Is due from from Man to Man.———Come, Lady, on;

The Altar now attends your maiden Vows;

Be thrifty of the Hour, the Day wears faſt.

[*Exeunt* MUSIDORUS, LYSANDER,
EUPHEMIA, *and* DELIA.

FIRST ARCADIAN.

Now with light Foot, to ſportive Meaſures beat,

Strike ev'ry ſprightly Note, that ere we join

In yonder hallow'd Grove, we to the Dance

May add new Graces, and avow our Zeal.

A DANCE *of* ARCADIANS.

After

After the Dance, *the* Chorus *repeated.*

Give the Hour to fober Pleafures ;

Cheerful Hearts are Life's beft Treafures :

Let the choral Song go round ;

Echo fhall our Joys refound.

[*Exeunt.*

SCENE— *A wild rocky Entrance to a Cave ; on one Side of which is feen a Wood.*

DORASTUS *enters from the Cave. After looking attentively around, he comes flowly forward.*

Hail ! to the Ev'ning Sun, which from the Weft

Empurples all the Sky, and this my Cave

Gilds with its parting Rays ; this mofs-grown Cave,

Long by my Footfteps worn !——for fince the Arms

Of the fell Spartans tore my Child away,

(Sole Pledge of a dear Union) with the Friend

To whom her dying Mother gave the Charge

To train her Infancy ; and ev'ry Hope

To

To trace their Fate is vain; I've fhun'd the Plain,

Nor mingled with the Gay.—In thefe lone Shades

I wake my Mind to Truth; and as the Stream

Of Life flows gently on, purfue that Peace

Philofophy infpires, and patient wait

Th' Appointment of the Gods.——But I muft hence—

The length'ning Shadows warn me now to feek

In the near Valley fuch fweet fmelling Flow'rs

As give their Perfumes to the Ev'ning Gale,

And ftrew them round yon vacant Tomb I've rear'd

To footh a Father's Sorrows.——There's in Grief

A melancholy Pleafure, which indulg'd,

Becalms the Soul;—and fuch this Tafk to me.——

O much-lamented Maid! if from this World

Efcap'd, thou fit'ft a Spirit in Air, accept

A Parent's pious Off'ring;—or if ftill

Thou draw'ft the Breath of Bondage, or art doom'd

To tread the flinty Ways of Life, may Heav'n

Give thee proportion'd Virtue!—Yet a while,

D

A tranfient

A tranſient Space, Time's friendly Hand ſhall guide

Each Suff'rer to his Reſt, and all our Cares

Shall melt to nothing, like the Morning Dew.

[Exit.

END OF THE FIRST ACT.

ACT

A C T   II.

A   R U R A L   S C E N E.

Enter LYSANDER, EUPHEMIA, DELIA, MUSIDORUS,
DAPHNE, *and* LAURA.

As they are all advancing from the End of the Stage, DAPHNE *and*
LAURA *sing the following*

D U E T.

HYMEN pleas'd your Faith furveys;
    All his peaceful Bleffings fhare!

Pureft Friendfhip crown your Days!

    Joy attend you, happy Pair!

L Y S A N D E R.

Thanks, courteous Fair-ones, Thanks; I little hop'd

Such Bride-maids for my Love; but you are all

As bounteous as your Skies; and your kind Care

Shall bind us both your Debtors.——You, good Shepherd,

                Who

Who with your Daughters at the Shrine of PAN

Have witnefs'd to our Vows, 'fhall fee I truft

That they were feal'd with Truth, and only join'd

Hearts of congenial Mould.

MUSIDORUS.

May circling Years

Still firmer bind them! and the Hand of Death

Alone diffolve this Union!

EUPHEMIA.

Heav'n fo grant!———

Moft freely Shepherd I accept your Grace,

And proffer'd Services ; wrapt in Delight

To meet already in this ftranger Land

Such hofpitable Smiles.

DAPHNE.

Nor here is feen

A Smile the Heart avows not; our plain Life

Difdains thofe Arts and Falfhoods, which they fay

Are practis'd by the Great-ones of the World.

Ambition

Ambition walks not here ; nor is here known

Envy, its fell Affociate.——Rural Cares

Employ the fleeting Day, and one firm Chain

Of focial Harmony unites us all.——

Our temp'rate Board gives Cheerfulnefs and Health ;

And there Contentment fits, and bids us fcorn

What cheated Man calls Luxury.

L A U R A.

Nor yet

Shall our calm Plains abufe your Hopes ; the Eye

As well as Mind is folac'd.——Nature blooms

In youthful Beauty round us, from her Urn

Scatt'ring unnumber'd Treafures.   Mark how glows

The vivid Landfcape ; and the burthen'd Earth

Pants with the gay Profufion.

E U P H E M I A.

A new World

Springs up before me.   See, Lysander, fee

What

What vary'd Sweets fhall ftrew our future Paths
Beneath this better Sun.

L Y S A N D E R.

Rooted I ftand,

And loft in Admiration thank the Gods
For all their Bounty to me; chief for Thee
Their nobleft Boon, thou Crown of my Defires!
Thou lovely Charmer!——O my Friends, excufe
A young Man's Tranfport; when you better know
This Maiden's Excellence, you will confefs
My Tongue no Flatt'rer——for fhe wears a Heart
So pure, fo fpotlefs, that it might be fhrin'd
In Cryftal, and have all its Movements fcann'd!

M U S I D O R U S.

My Bofom fhares your Tranfport.——Gentle Lady,
Beneath the Umbrage of yon tufted Trees,
Which fhade the Margin of the azure Stream
That fteals along its Side, our Dwelling ftands,
Ruftic and fimple; thick around it fhoots

The

The flaunting Woodbine; and each fragrant Flow'r

Adorns the verdant Scene.——There I've prepar'd

A cheerful Welcome;——all our rural Sports

My Daughters shall relate, and teach you too,

If so you like, to tend our fleecy Folds;

For all are Shepherds here.

EUPHEMIA.

Something but now,

As o'er the Lawn we pass'd, LAURA discours'd

Of a grey Hermit, whose religious Life

Gain'd him such Love, that each ARCADIAN deem'd

His Blessing prosp'rous; fain on this Day's Act

Would I implore it.

MUSIDORUS.

Lady, he you mean

Dwells at the mossy Foot of yonder Rock,

The good DORASTUS; Shepherd once himself,

And Master still of many a Flock; but he,

Long from our Plains sequester'd, mourns retir'd

A Loss

A Lofs that weighs his grey Hairs down.——All here
View him with filial Love ; for he's to all
A Friend, a Father.——Thither I'll conduct you
As homeward now we pafs.

LYSANDER.

We will attend ;

Yet tarry but a Space, while from thofe Trees
Of cluft'ring Rofes that invite the Touch
I pluck fome crimfon Buds, and twift a Wreath
For my Euphemia's Brow ; fhe has not yet
Receiv'd her bridal Garland.

[*Exit.*

EUPHEMIA.

On this Bank

Await we his Return. Sit, my fair Maids ;
And Delia, calm the Flutt'rings of my Heart
By fome foft Strain.——Give me that cheering Song
Aranthe fo much lov'd.

DELIA.

D E L I A.

       'Tis well devis'd,
Nor foreign to the Moment.——I obey.

S O N G.

All the Splendor which Wealth can difplay
    Is fo vain, that it quickly muft cloy;
Like a Bubble, it foon melts away,
    If HOPE does not heighten the Joy.

Sweet Paffion! without thee, the Soul
    In the Midft of Fruition would tire;
Into Times yet unborn thou canft roll,
    And expand on the Wings of Defire.

It was HOPE that firft planted my Vine,
    And its Clufters luxurioufly fpread;
Rear'd my Fig-tree whofe Branches intwine,
    And fo gratefully fhadow my Head.

HOPE

[26]

Hope comforts the Mourner's fad State,

 Sooths the Wretch who is ftruggling with Pain,

Bids the Captive fupport his hard Fate,

 And to Home turns his Eyes back again.

Bright Charmer! ah! live in my Breaft,

 Round my Temples thy Garland ftill bind;

Thou fhalt calm all my Sorrows to Reft,

 And cheer with thy Sunfhine my Mind.

E U P H E M I A.

Kind Delia, take my Thanks.——I feel the Truth

Thy Strain infpires; for fee Lysander comes,

Who round the little Region of my Heart

Bids Hope triumphant live.

Lysander *re-enters, with a Chaplet of Rofes in his Hand.*

L Y S A N D E R.

    Euphemia, wear

This blooming Wreath, in Honor of the Day,

         And

And as an Emblem of our twin'd Affections.——

[*Prefents her the Chaplet.*

This hath a tranfient Date, but they I truft

Shall never know Decay.——Now let us fpeed

To feek the Hermit's Cave; good Shepherd on.

[*Exeunt.*

The Scene opening difcovers a Wood. In the Middle of the Stage is a MONUMENT, *with the Statue of a Nymph lying on it. Upon its Bafe appears this Infcription, in large Charaɛters,*

I TOO WAS AN ARCADIAN.

D O R A S T U S *is feen ftanding near the Tomb, with a Bafket of Flowers in his Hand, finging the following*

A I R.

My Woes, O Mem'ry! ceafe to trace;

Ah! curfe no more the SPARTAN Race!

Come meek-ey'd Patience, calm my Mind,

And make it to its Fate refign'd.——

This fancy'd Form, this empty Tomb

Relieves the Rigour of my Doom.

E 2 *Enter*

Enter MUSIDORUS, LYSANDER, EUPHEMIA,
DELIA, DAPHNE, *and* LAURA.

MUSIDORUS.

Behold the good old Man!——On the ſtill Air

How ſweetly floats his plaintive Voice!——Beſide

This Wood he dwells, and here at ſetting Sun

Sings his accuſtom'd Dirge, as Mem'ry drops

A Sigh o'er happier Scenes that Time hath clos'd.

LYSANDER.

Say, what yon Pile which he beſtrews with Flow'rs?

It ſeems a Tomb, and that fair ſculptur'd Form

Declares it ſuch ; as does the Epitaph,

" *I too was an Arcadian.*"

MUSIDORUS.

He bewails

A Daughter torn away, on whom he built

The Comfort of his Age ; it is for her

This mournful Pile is rear'd, theſe Rites perform'd.——

But

But foft!—A Moment ends them ; let us not

Invade his Privacy.

> [*They keep retired on one Side of the Stage.*

DORASTUS *continues the Air, ſtrewing the Flowers round the Tomb.*

> Gentle Spirit, Peace be thine !
>
> This fad Office ftill be mine ;
>
> Thefe fond Marks of Love receive,
>
> All a drooping Sire can give.

During the Song, LYSANDER *diſcourſes with* MUSIDORUS ;—EUPHEMIA, *with* DAPHNE *and* LAURA. *She often fixes her Eyes on the Monument, with Marks of Emotion.*

The Song ended, they advance.

MUSIDORUS.

> Good Ev'n, DORASTUS,

And heard be all thy Orifons !——Behold

I bring with me a Pair, who even now

At yonder confecrated Altar feal'd

The Bond of wedded Faith.——Far is their Home,

Beyond the Southern Mountains ; but Defire

To

To vifit thefe our Plains hath urg'd their Steps

Hither, to fojourn with us.——Lo! they fue

Your Grace and Welcome; and will prove, I judge,

Worthy your Courtefy.——Their bridal Bed

My Daughters have prepar'd; and I myfelf

Shall be their this Night's Hoft; a fecret Impulfe

Hath won me to their Service.

LYSANDER.

Strangers here,

Each Mark of Hofpitality muft charm;

And footh to fay, this our kind Patron's Care

Hath far outftrip'd my Hope.——Might we obtain

Thy Pray'rs, refpected Hermit, nothing then

Remains to crown our Fortune.

DORASTUS.

If the Blefling

Of an old Man by many a Sorrow worn,

And bow'd by many a Year, can aught avail,

O take it, freely take it.——May the Act

Of

Of this fair Day be profper'd ! may a Length

Of Happinefs be yours ! a virtuous Race

To both endear the World ! and all your Paths,

Your Ev'ning Paths of Life, be fpread with Flow'rs

That never grew in mine !

LYSANDER.

Ah ! much I grieve

That your's have prov'd uneven !——For your Wifhes

Count me your Debtor.——My EUPHEMIA too,

My Bride fhall thank you ; for her Heart is gentle,

And grateful as the Flow'r that pays with Sweets

The genial Summer's Bounty !——

As he turns to EUPHEMIA, *he finds her looking towards the Tomb with a melancholy Attention.*

Ha ! my Love,

Whence this Amaze ? why doft thou bend thy Sight

On yonder Tomb ? and wherefore on thy Brow

Sits a defcriptive Sorrow, that hath drank

The Luftre of thine Eyes, and damp'd the Joy

Which

Which fparkled there but now ?—Say, why is this ?
What the ftrange Caufe ?

EUPHEMIA.

The Caufe is in myfelf;
O my LYSANDER ! I have fool'd my Senfe
With vifionary Hope, and now awake
To meet my Error.

LYSANDER.

Nay ! explain, EUPHEMIA.

EUPHEMIA.

This good Man's Sigh has op'd my Eyes; this Scene
Of Death has undeceiv'd me.——Blind to think
That there was any Ground where Mortals tread
On which Affliction walks not !——Ev'ry Clime
Engenders human Woe ; and fam'd ARCADIA
Is pregnant with the fame difaftrous Fortune
That other Regions know.

DORASTUS.

Our Life, fair Lady,

Muft

Muſt needs be chequer'd thus.

LYSANDER.

Alas! my Love,

Let us enjoy the Good, nor with vain Search

Anticipate Misfortune ; come it will,

Though Wiſdom ſtand as Guard ; and e'en theſe Shades

Muſt ſometimes own its Pow'r.

EUPHEMIA.

Miſtaken Maid!

Is this the Land where Pleaſure only reign'd ?

Was it for this I pac'd ſo long a Way ?

Abandon'd SPARTA ? and ſo far allur'd

Thy wand'ring Steps LYSANDER, here to meet

The Face of Sorrow ?——Where is that Content

ARANTHE boaſted ? Where that Peace, ſhe ſaid

Should greet our Coming?——Ah! could ſhe delude

That Hope ſhe ſo long nouriſh'd ?

DORASTUS.

Heard I aright ?

F

Or did falfe Sounds abufe me ?——Spake you not

Of SPARTA, and ARANTHE, courteous Lady?

Pray you fay on; for to my Ear you utter'd

A Name well known.——ARANTHE ! knew you her ?

And lives fhe yet ?

LYSANDER.

Ah no! fhe is no more!

With pious Hand thefe Maidens clos'd her Eyes,

Bathing her Corfe with Tears.

EUPHEMIA.

In her I loft

The beft of Women, whofe indulgent Care

No Time fhall wear away.——Her lateft Wifh

Was I fhould feek ARCADIA, where herfelf

Had fometime known a happier Deftiny

Than SPARTA's Walls afforded.

DORASTUS.

You are then

Her Daughter doubtlefs ; you perhaps have oft

Heard

Heard her relate- - -

EUPHEMIA.

Good Hermit, you miftake;

I am no Child of her's, though many a Year

Such I was deem'd, till her laft Breath unveil'd

The Error, and declar'd I was a Pledge

Inftrufted to her Care in infant Years,

By whom was unexplain'd, for Death's cold Grafp

Broke off th' unfinifh'd Tale,——and I had walk'd

The World a friendlefs Orphan, and alone,

But for this virtuous Youth, to whom I've giv'n

That Love his Merit claim'd.——But why on me

Is caft that Look of Eagernefs ?—Why heaves

Thy lab'ring Bofom thus ? or whence thofe Tears

That tremble in thine Eye ?

DORASTUS.

O Nature !--Nature !

Who with thy pow'rful, and invifible Hand

Shak'ft my whole Frame with Tumult,—can I think

This

This Conflict, thefe Forebodings of a Father
Are rais'd, or felt in vain ?——The Stroke's too great !
Pray you your Arm a Moment. ——Yes—it muft—
Thofe Features wear the radiant Hue of Truth !—
There cannot be Deceit.——It is—It is.
My long-loft Child reftor'd.——

EUPHEMIA.

All-ruling Gods !
Have ye upheld me through the Maze of Life
Unknowing, and unknown, in this far Land
To guide me to a Parent ?

LYSANDER.

All 's explain'd ;
This was ARANTHE's Meaning, this the Caufe
She urg'd fo ftrong your Coming, hoping ftill
Some Chance might bring about this bleft Event
Th' indulgent Gods have profper'd.

DORASTUS.

Gen'rous Youth !

Whofe

Whofe Graces have endear'd thee to my Child,

Whofe Truth and Friendfhip won her, let my Arms

Embrace thee as a Son.———A Father's Blefling,

Pour'd from a Heart with Gratitude o'ercome,

Shall now enforce the reft.———Alas! too quick

My Spirits bound!———Prithee refolve my Mind

A few fond Queftions more.

[They withdraw to the Bottom of the Stage.

MUSIDORUS.

See, my Children,

The virtuous ftill are happy!—This is fhe

So long-reputed dead, for whom was rear'd

The Statue, and the Tomb; for whom thefe Shades

So oft' have echo'd with a Father's Sighs;

Sighs now repaid with Tranfports!

LAURA.

Nor in vain

Have we intwin'd the feftive Wreath. This Night

Shall focial Pleafure beam from ev'ry Eye,

And

And Sounds of Joy be heard along the Vale.

D A P H N E.

See where returning from the hallow'd Grove
The Shepherds crofs the Plain.   I'll be myfelf
Of this Event the Harbinger; 'twill prove
Moft welcome to them all.

[Exit.

DORASTUS, LYSANDER, EUPHEMIA, *and* **DELIA,**
come forward.

D O R A S T U S.

Enough, enough;

My ftormy Life at laft finks to a Calm.
Come Death now when it will, I'll meet it fmiling,
Upheld by this lov'd Pair.

L Y S A N D E R.

Long live to fee

Our mutual Happinefs! and be repaid
In the bright Virtues of your new-found Daughter
The Suff'rings you've endur'd!

DORASTUS.

DORASTUS.

Great Providence!

How juft are all thy Ways!——Never let Man,

Howe'er he be diftrefs'd, abandon Hope;

For in the Moment when the Cloud is blackeft,

When the big Storm rolls loudeft o'er his Head,

The Hand of Heav'n perhaps fupports his Steps,

And guides him back to Peace!——'Twas but this Morn,

Stung with Remembrance of my former Woes,

I curs'd the Sons of SPARTA; ere Day clofe

A SPARTAN Hand leads back the Child I loft,

And quite atones the Wrongs his Country did me!

EUPHEMIA.

Juftly I ftand reprov'd.——Henceforth I'll own

Each Murmur is a Crime, and Difcontent

Ingratitude to Heav'n.

DORASTUS.

Forbear to think

This Earth can teem Perfection; far beyond

Thofe

Thofe azure Rocks that kifs the floping Sky

A happier Region lies, to which compar'd

Our Spot, is as the dank and tainted Gale

To th' unfully'd Breath of Morning.——There the Toils

Of lab'ring Virtue ceafe! and thither oft'

She turns her patient Eye, and feeks her Crown!——

'Tis there EUPHEMIA, and 'tis there alone

Perfection may be hop'd; on this Side, all

Is mutable and frail!

E U P H E M I A.

      Yet 'tis not ftrange

The Mind that's tutor'd to expect too much

Should figh at Difappointment.

D O R A S T U S.

      That, my Child,

Is Life's grand Error;—we delude ourfelves,

And charge the Cheats of FANCY to the World.——

Man in his vifionary Hour conceives

Joys never deftin'd for him, then fits down

In

In fullen Difcontent, to think he lofes

That which he ne'er poffefs'd.——Go, wifer you

My Children, curb your Wifhes, tafte with Thanks

That Good the Gods allot you ; and remember,

Howe'er our Paths are chequer'd by Misfortune,

Life ftill has many Pleafures for the Virtuous.

MUSIDORUS.

The neighb'ring Swains, whom DELIA has inform'd

Of what has chanc'd, with Looks of Tranfport hafte

To greet your happier Fortune.

A Number of ARCADIANS *enter with* DAPHNE, *and furround* DORASTUS *with Marks of Congratulation.*

DORASTUS.

Ah ! how fweet

Their Steps who fpeak of Peace !——I have, my Friends,

A Heart that reads your Purpofe in your Eye,

And regifters your Love——A Heart, the Gods

Have quite o'erwhelm'd with Mercy !——Thanks to all

Who fhare with me this Joy; and double Thanks

To thee, kind MUSIDORUS, whom this Night

We all will fojourn with, and cheer the Board

Thy lib'ral Hand has fpread.——Rich Flocks, and Herds,

And wide-fpread Paftures, fhall be giv'n to-morrow

In Dowry with this Maid.——You DELIA too

Shall now become my Care.——Let us away.

The Ev'ning Star is ris'n,——and as we pafs

Let all our choral Youth their Voices join

In Notes that deep-felt Gratitude infpires.

C H O R U S.

Mighty PAN ! to thee we owe

All the Happinefs we know ;—

Let our Lives ftill peaceful glide ;

Give us Virtue for our Guide.

[*Exeunt.*

E P I L O G U E.

EPILOGUE.

Mortals, who this Drama view,
Own you not its Moral true?———
Virtuous Minds fhould ne'er defpair ;
They are Heav'n's peculiar Care,
Who teaches fuff'ring Man to know
HOPE'S THE COUNTERPOISE OF WOE.

But if HOPE *unlicens'd reigns,*
Wildly feeks ideal Plains,
Pictures Joys it ne'er can meet,
Paths ne'er trod by human Feet ;
Then, ah! then expect to find
ARCADIA'S ONLY IN THE MIND.

THE END.